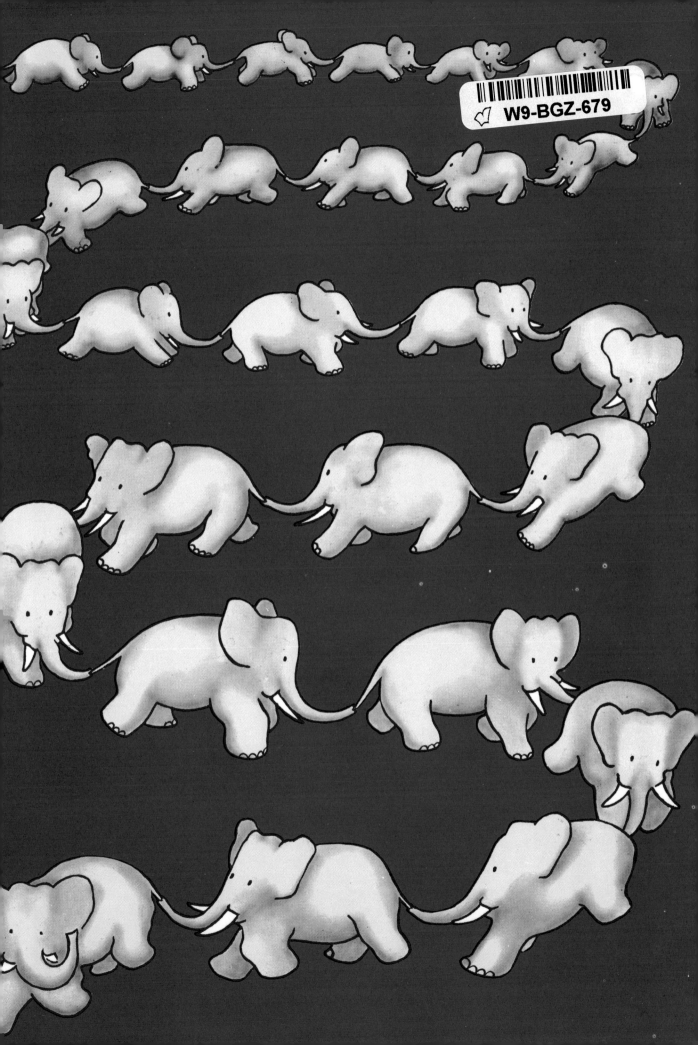

Nanci,

This is book 2. It's just as good as the first. If you really like these maybe you can tell your mom and I'll get you a few more. Merry Christmas!

Love always,
Aunt Cindy
&
Steven

12-1979

JEAN DE BRUNHOFF

THE TRAVELS
of
BABAR

Translated from the French by Merle S. Haas
Random House – New York

The Babar Books

The Story of Babar
The Travels of Babar
Babar the King
Babar and Zéphir
Babar and His Children
Babar and Father Christmas
Babar's Cousin: That Rascal Arthur
Babar's Picnic
Babar's Fair
Babar and the Professor
Babar's Castle
Babar's French Lessons
Babar Comes to America
Babar's Spanish Lessons
Babar Loses His Crown
Babar's Trunk
Babar's Birthday Surprise
Babar's Other Trunk
Babar Visits Another Planet
Meet Babar and His Family
Babar's Bookmobile
Babar and the Wully-Wully
Babar Saves the Day

In this story of the little elephant who is beloved by millions of children, Babar and his bride Celeste start on an aerial honeymoon. Their balloon is wrecked on a cannibal island; but the most famous little elephant in the world again triumphs over great odds.

This title was originally cataloged by the Library of Congress as follows:
De Brunhoff, Jean   The Travels of Babar; trans. from the French by Merle S. Haas. Random House ©1961   48p col illus   1 Picture books for children
I. Haas, Merle S. trans. II. Title   E
ISBN 0-394-80576-3   0-394-90576-8 (lib. bdg.)

Babar, the young King of the elephants, and his wife, Queen Celeste, have just left for their wedding trip in a balloon.

"Good-by! See you soon!" cry the elephants as they watch the balloon rise and drift away.

Arthur, Babar's little cousin, still waves his beret. Old Cornelius, who is chief over all the elephants when the King is away, anxiously sighs: "I do hope they won't have any accidents!"

The country of the elephants is now far away.
The balloon glides noiselessly in the sky. Babar
and Celeste admire the landscape below. What
a beautiful journey! The air is balmy, the wind
is gentle. There is the ocean, the big blue ocean.

Blown out over the sea by the wind, the balloon is suddenly caught by a violent storm. Babar and Celeste tremble with fear and cling with all their might to the basket of the balloon.

By extraordinary good fortune, just as the balloon is about to fall into the sea, a final puff of wind blows it on an island where it flattens out and collapses.

"You aren't hurt, Celeste, are you?" Babar inquires anxiously. "No! Well then look, we are saved!"

Leaving the wrecked balloon on the beach, Babar and Celeste pick up their belongings and go off to seek shelter.

Having found a quiet spot, they take off their clothes. Celeste hangs them up to dry, while Babar lights a good fire and prepares breakfast.

Babar and Celeste settle themselves comfort-
ably. They have set up their tent and, sitting
on some large stones, they eat with relish an
excellent rice broth well-sweetened and cooked
to perfection. "We are not so badly off on this
island," says Babar.

After breakfast, while Babar explores the surrounding country, Celeste, left alone, falls sound asleep.

Just then, the inhabitants of the island, fierce and savage cannibals, suddenly discover her.

"What kind of strange beast is this?" they say to one another. "We have never seen anything like it. Its meat must be very tender. Let's creep up quietly and catch it while it sleeps."

The cannibals have succeeded in tying up
Celeste with the clothesline on which the clothes
were drying. Some dance with joy, while others
have great fun trying on the stolen garments.
Celeste sighs sadly, she thinks soon she will be
eaten. She does not yet see Babar, who returns
just in time to save her!

In the twinkling of an eye, Babar has unbound
Celeste. They both hurl themselves on the cannibals. Some are wounded, others take flight; all
are terrified.

Only a few courageous ones still resist. But they are thinking: "These big animals are certainly terribly strong and their hides are mighty tough!"

After having chased off the savages, Babar and Celeste rest themselves on the seashore. Suddenly, right in front of them a whale comes to the surface and spouts. Babar gets up immediately and says:

"Good morning, Mrs. Whale, I am Babar, King of the elephants, and here is my wife Celeste. We have had a balloon accident and have fallen here on this island. Could you help us to get away?"

"I am delighted to make your acquaintance,"
answers the whale, "and I will be very happy if
I can be of service to you. I am just leaving to
visit my family in the Arctic Ocean. I will drop
you wherever you like. Quick, get on my back
and hold tight so you don't slip off. Are you
ready? Get set. Let's go!"

A few days later, a little weary, they are rest-
ing on a reef. Just then a school of little fish
swims by.

"I am going to eat up some of these," says the
whale. "I'll be back in a minute." And she dives
down after them.

The whale has not come back! While eating the little fish, she completely forgot her new friends. She is a giddy, thoughtless creature.

"We were better off on the cannibal island. What will become of us now?" weeps poor Celeste. Babar does his best to comfort her.

After hours and hours spent on their little reef, without even a drop of fresh water, they finally spy a ship passing quite near them. She is a big steamer with three funnels. Babar and Celeste call out and yell as loudly as they can, but no one hears them. They try signaling with their trunks and with their arms. Oh, will they attract someone's attention?

They have been seen! A lifeboat rescues them
while the excited passengers all watch.

A week later, the huge ship

steams slowly into a big harbor.

All the passengers go down the gangplank. Babar and Celeste would like to follow too but they are not allowed to. They have lost their crowns during the storm, so no one will believe that they are actually King and Queen of the elephants, and the Captain of the ship orders them locked up in the ship's stables.

"They give us straw to sleep on!" cries Babar angrily. "We are fed hay, as though we were donkeys! The door is locked! I've had enough of this, I'm going to smash everything."

"Be quiet, I beg you," says Celeste, "I hear someone. It is the Captain coming into the stable. Let's be good so he'll let us out."

"Here are my elephants," says the Captain to
the famous animal trainer, Fernando, who is with
him. "I cannot keep them on my ship; I give
them to you for your circus."

Fernando thanks the Captain and leads away
his two new pupils.

"Be patient, Babar," whispers Celeste, "we will
not remain long with the circus. We will get back
to our native land again somehow and see Cornelius and little Arthur."

Now just at this time, back in the elephants' country, little Arthur has had a mischievous idea. While Rataxes the rhinoceros was having a quiet siesta, Arthur tied a big firecracker to his tail without waking him. The firecracker explodes with a terrific bang and Rataxes leaps up into the air. Arthur, the scamp, laughs until he nearly chokes. It is really a very **mean trick**.

Rataxes is furious. Cornelius, very worried, goes
to find him and says:

"My dear fellow, I am so sorry. Arthur will be
severely punished. He begs for your forgiveness."

"Get away, old Cornelius," grumbles Rataxes.
"Don't speak to me of that scoundrel, Arthur. You
elephants may think you have made fun of me but
just wait—you'll soon see!"

"What will he do?" wonders Cornelius. "I feel
very uneasy; he is revengeful and mean. Ah! If only
Babar were here!"

But Babar is now far away playing the trumpet

while Celeste dances in Fernando's circus.

One day the circus comes to the town where
Babar, when he was young, had met his friend
the Old Lady. So, at night, while Fernando is in
bed, Babar and Celeste escape and go to find her,
for he has never forgotten her.

Babar finds the house easily and rings the bell.
The Old Lady awakes, puts on her wrapper, steps
out on her balcony and calls:

"Who's there?"

"Babar and Celeste," they answer her.

The Old Lady is overjoyed. She has really be-
lieved she would never see them again. Babar and
Celeste are happy, too, for they will never have
to go back to the circus. Soon they will be able
to rejoin Arthur and Cornelius. The Old Lady
has promised to help them.

The Old Lady lends Celeste a nightgown and provides Babar with a pair of pajamas. They have just awakened after a sound sleep. Now they are having breakfast in bed for they are still quite tired after all their adventures.

At the circus, their escape has just been dis-
covered.

"Stop! Thief! My elephants have been stolen!"
cries the excited Fernando.

"Little ones, oh little ones, where are you hiding?" the clowns repeat, and look everywhere for
them.

Babar and Celeste will not be caught again.
Here they are on their way to the station with
the Old Lady. They need a few days' rest before
returning to their own land. So the three of them
are going to the mountains to enjoy the fresh air
and try a little skiing.

Now Babar and Celeste have packed away their skis and said good-by to the mountains. They are leaving by plane to return home. The Old Lady accompanies them. Babar has invited her, as he is anxious to show her his beautiful country and the great forest where one always hears the birds singing.

They have landed. The airplane has gone back.
Babar and Celeste are speechless with surprise.
Where are Cornelius, Arthur, and the other elephants? A few broken trees! Is that all that is left
of the great forest? There are no more flowers,
no more birds. Babar and Celeste are very sad
and weep as they see their ruined country. The
Old Lady understands their grief.

"What is going on here?" inquiries Babar, who has found the other elephants at last.

"Alas!" replies Cornelius. "The rhinoceroses have declared war on us. They came led by Rataxes who wanted to catch Arthur and make mincemeat of him! We tried bravely to protect the little fellow, but the rhinoceroses were too strong for us. We do not know how to drive them off."

"This is indeed bad news," says Babar, "but let's not give up."

But real war is not a joke, and many of the elephants have been wounded. Celeste and the Old Lady take care of them with great devotion. The Old Lady is especially good at this, as she used to be a trained nurse. Babar and some of the soldiers who have recovered have gone back to the front with Cornelius to join the elephant army. The rhinoceroses are preparing to attack. A big battle will soon begin!

Here is the camp of the rhinoceroses. The soldiers are awaiting orders, and think: "We will once again defeat the elephants, then the war will be over and we can all go home." Spiteful old Rataxes maliciously says to his friend General Pamir: "Hah! Hah! Hah! Pretty soon we will tweak the ears of this young King Babar and punish that rascal Arthur."

Here is the camp of the elephants. They have
all found new courage. And now Babar has a
bright idea:

He disguises his biggest soldiers, painting their
tails bright red, and near their tails on either side
he paints large, frightening eyes. Arthur sets to
work making wigs. He works as hard as he can
so he'll be forgiven for causing all this trouble.

The day of the battle, at just the right moment the disguised elephants come out of hiding. And Babar's bright idea succeeds!

The rhinoceroses think they are monsters and, terrified, they retreat in great disorder. King Babar is a mighty fine general.

The rhinoceroses have fled and are still running. Pamir and Rataxes are prisoners, and hang their heads in shame. What a glorious day for the elephants! In chorus they all cry:

"Bravo, Babar–Bravo! Victory! Victory! The war is over! How perfectly splendid!"

The next day before all the elephants, Babar
and Celeste, having put on their royal garments
and their new crowns, reward the Old Lady who
has been so good to them and has cared so well
for the wounded. They give her eleven singing
canaries and a cunning little monkey.

After the ceremony, Babar, Celeste and the Old Lady sit and chat under the palm trees. "And what are we going to do next?" asks the Old Lady.

"I am going to try to rule my kingdom wisely," answers Babar, "and if you will remain with us, you can help me make my subjects happy."

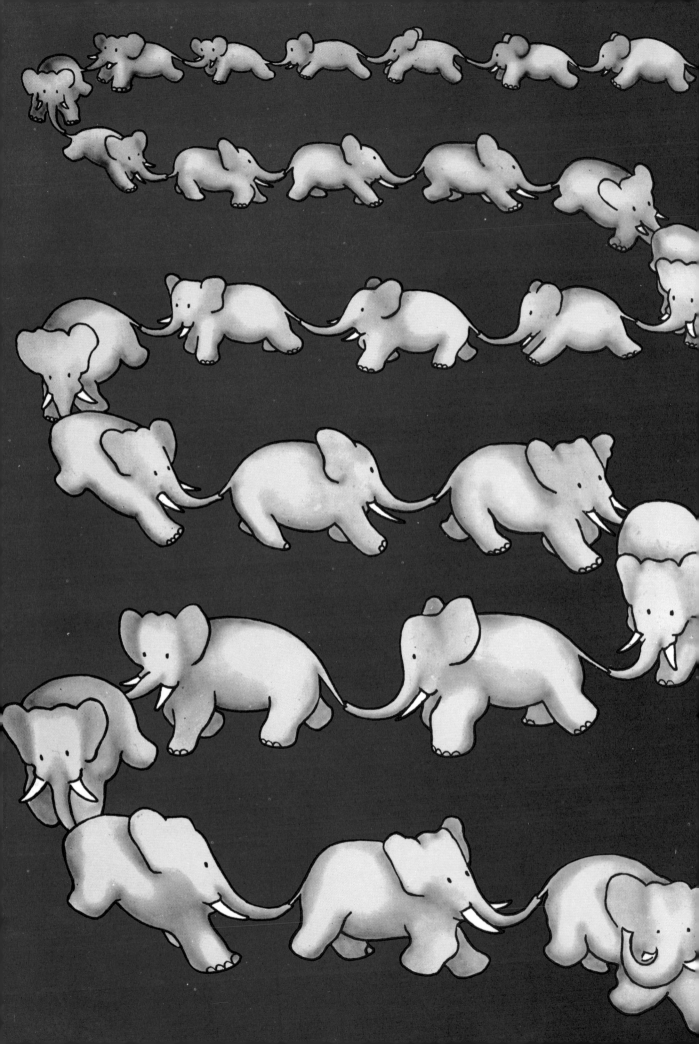